KU-035-373

Mrs Webster

The Cry of the Wolf

the Wolf

and other

short stories

selected by
Stewart Ross

Illustrations by Katy Jenkins, Age 13, Buckler's Mead Community School, Somerset.

The Cry of the Wolf

and other

short stories

An anthology of winning stories from the 2008 – 2009
World Book Day Short Story competition

In association

Published in 2009 by Evans Brothers Limited
2A Portman Mansions
Chiltern Street
London W1U 6NR

© Evans Brothers Limited 2009

All rights reserved. No part of this publication may be reproduced, stored in a retrieval system or transmitted in any form or by any means, electronic, mechanical, photocopying, recording or otherwise, without prior permission of the Publishers.

British Library Cataloguing in Publication Data
A catalogue record for this book is available from the British Library

ISBN: 9780237538231

Editor: Bryony Jones
Designers: Rebecca Fox, Evans
Jo Kennedy, Us2Design

FOREWORD

I find it difficult to believe what I have been
reading. These stories are by students, children
still at school? Impossible! Many of them are
better, vastly better than adult equivalents
published in magazines. Anyone wanting to know
what the young are thinking nowadays, how
their minds are working, is urged to read this
terrific collection – and stand amazed at its skill,
inventiveness, vitality, sensitivity, wit and painful
honesty. I am honoured, truly, to have been asked
to make the selection.

Mind you, it was an almost impossible
task. Much to my dismay, I was unable to include
the 1984-style futuristic nightmare of Katharine
Crossman, or Alexandra Pringle's delightful
'Intruder', Sophie Kippen's intriguing peep inside
the mind of Hamlet or Hattie Casey's glimpse of
a green new world. So, if your story is not here,
please remember that this is not a collection of *the*

best stories – although they are all excellent – but a selection *from* the best fifty or so. Our aim has been to produce a broad cross-section of the finest modern writing by young people, representing all regions, ages and styles. As a result, and because we are limited to just eleven examples, we have had to leave many splendid pieces of writing on one side.

In making our final selection we did come across a number of the stories that were sadly over-written, full of convoluted sentences and clogged with superfluous adjectives. In a bid to fight against this, I link arms with George Orwell. In 'Politics and the English Language' (1946) this master of modern prose suggested: 'Never use a long word where a short one will do' and 'If it is possible to cut a word out, always cut it out.' Although Orwell was not talking about what he called 'the literary use of language', his advice holds pretty good for most of us attempting to communicate effectively with our fellow human beings - especially if we bear in mind his last rule: 'Break any of these rules sooner than say anything outright barbarous!'

Two aspects of the top fifty stories

astonished me. One was the degree of intellectual and emotional maturity they showed (try Alice Glebocki's 'Crazy Woman', for example); the other was the sophisticated way several authors played with the opening sentences they had been given. It was as if they had said to themselves, 'Hey, that's a pretty naff beginning. How can I turn it into something original?' Hence Poppy Donaldson's charming shrouded cage tale.

Last year I singled out my favourite story. There are too many gems for that to be possible this time, but I would like to congratulate Oxford High School for consistently finding so many writers of exceptional ability. Once again, huge votes of thanks are due to the heroic teachers who continue to inspire, assist and instruct our young writers, and to World Book Day and the Evans Publishing Group for organising a remarkable venture. Together they have enabled this precious anthology of sparkling talent to appear. Above all, though, our thanks and congratulations must go to the young authors themselves. The future is bright indeed.

Stewart Ross
Blean, 2009

Drawing by Sarah Jenkins, Age 11, Buckler's Mead Community School, Somerset.

ACKNOWLEDGEMENTS

Once again we have been overwhelmed by the support shown for the competition.

So thank you to all the young writers who have put pen to paper - or more likely, fingers to keyboards - and to the young illustrators who have sent us some delightful pictures. It has been a privilege for us to read and review your work.

Congratulations to our talented winners. And if you didn't win this year, keep at it – maybe next year will be your year!

Thank you too, to all the teachers, librarians and parents who encouraged our entrants to write so creatively for this competition.

Special thanks are also due to the authors who provided first lines, and to their publishers, with an honourable mention for Stewart Ross who has freely given so much of his time to read the shortlist of entries and write the foreword. His tireless enthusiasm for the art of writing and the importance of books for children is an inspiration to everyone.

Thank you also to Cathy Schofield of World Book Day, Kate Bostock of the Publishers Association, and Truda Spruyt and Chris Baker from Colman Getty for supporting the competition so wholeheartedly once more.

Log on to **www.worldbookday.com** or **www.evansbooks.co.uk** for news of next year's competition.

CONTENTS

As the cry of the wolf echoed over the forest, the fire went out and Beck was left in darkness. He reached for his knife, hurriedly shoved it inside his backpack and started running...

Bear Grylls

Wolf

by Beth Cadwalladr

As the cry of the wolf echoed over the forest, the fire went out and Beck was left in darkness. He reached for his knife, hurriedly shoved it inside his backpack and started running... He followed the call, his bare feet pounding against the forest floor. When he finally reached the clearing, he saw to his amazement who had summoned him.

'He-who-runs-swiftly-in-moonlight!' Beck cried in astonishment. He knelt and touched his forehead to the ground in respect.

'Greeting-He-who-walks-on-two-legs-you-must-come.'

'Why?'

'You-are-healer-we-fight.'

'What?!' Beck was so astonished that he spoke out loud, something that he had not done for months. There was no need of it running with the wolves. He stared in bewilderment at the elder before him.

'Why-we-fight? I-thought-that-there-was-peace-in-the-forest-ever-since-the-war.'

'Not-all-two-legged-ones-honour-agreement-they-take-cubs-we-fight.'

Beck's mind was reeling. He had only been about two years old when the last war had taken place. The humans had been mistreating the planet for years, and as global warming reached fever pitch, the animals of the world had made alliances and fought to take control of the world that the humans could not look after.

Beck couldn't remember his parents. He assumed that they had been killed in the war. His earliest memory was sleeping in the forest having run from a horde of wild dogs, and being awoken by someone who then took him home. He had no idea how old she had been, because he could not remember her face. The only things he remembered about her were the scar that ran down the entire length of her right arm, the voice that was as sweet as a nightingale's, and the wolf's fang that she wore round her neck.

He had lived with her for about a year, until one moonlit night, instead of putting him to bed, she had led him into the forest that she had forbidden him to enter, laid him down, and sung what he thought was a lullaby. He knew now that she had been calling the wolves. Beck thought that he must have fallen asleep, because the next thing he knew he was alone in the forest. That was when they came.

He had been terrified when the gleaming yellow eyes had first appeared out of the darkness, when he first saw their razor sharp claws and their jagged teeth. He had seen what those terrible things could do.

'Who-are-you?' he had cried in the wild-speech that the woman had spoken to him in. It was a curious thing, wild-speech. She had told him that there was a part of his mind in which he could place thoughts and messages that he wanted her to hear. She had said that that part of his mind was shared with all others who could use wild-speech, so any thoughts he put in there would appear in the minds of the people and animals who could use it. Beck now knew that humans who could access this part of their minds were incredibly rare.

Ever since then Beck had run with the pack. They were the greatest pack in the forest. Their pack leader was a forest elder. He-who-runs-swiftly-in-moonlight, and the golden eagle, She-who-flies-high-over-mountaintops, were known as the mother and father of the forest. Beck was important to the pack leader. They called him 'The Healer' ever since a wolf had been shot by an arrow. Beck had removed the arrow and washed the wound, and he had used leaves to bandage the injured leg to a splint.

Although Beck was proud of this position in the pack, he felt honoured to be asked to fight alongside them. Then he realised the problem.

'But-how-will-I-fight? I-have-no-claws-nor-any-teeth-worth-speaking-of.'

'We-find-this-by-place-where-two-legs-dwell. You-use-it.'

19

Another wolf emerged from the trees. He carried a long object in his mouth. He dropped it at Beck's feet, and watched as Beck slowly examined the wickedly sharp scimitar, gleaming in the moonlight.

***

The battle was *sick*. Sick and twisted, and Beck just wanted to forget it forever. He watched as his pack brothers fell on all sides. He barely knew what was happening as the scimitar slashed again and again. The blade still gleamed, but it was not with moonlight. It was with blood.

The ambush that they had planned had fallen to pieces when some of his pack brothers, barely more than cubs, had grown excited, and ran to the front howling with delight. People swarmed in on them, and now they were fighting for their lives. The enormous building that they had been attacking remained unpenetrated. The guards outside the gates would not let anything pass through alive.

'Listen!'

Beck felt a tug at the back of his mind as he heard the thought. Every creature in the battle would be hearing it.

'He-who-strikes-strongly-with-claws-and-He-who-hunts-with-great-skill-attack-guards, and-He-who-walks-on-two-legs-go-past-into-two-legs-dwelling. Fell-guards-inside-let-others-in-we-find-cubs-and-take-them-back-to-forest. Others-let-no-two-

legs-see-now-go.'

Beck took a deep breath. This was his moment. It was now or never.

***

When two wolves hurled themselves at the guards and began fighting furiously, Beck ran. He dodged the guards and ran through the gates and into the courtyard beyond. A makeshift camp for the wounded had been set up there. Hundreds of men lay on straw pallets, groaning as the overworked attendants rushed around. No one seemed to notice him as he made for the door to the building itself. Beck felt ill after seeing what that wonderful gleaming scimitar could do. As soon as he got inside Beck looked around the grand entrance hall, and realised just how vast the building was. He closed his eyes and listened for the cubs he knew were in there somewhere. But the cries he could hear were not cries of sadness. They were cries of joy. Beck belted up the staircase to his left, following the thoughts. At last he burst into a tower room where he saw something extraordinary.

A young girl, about twelve years old, was sitting on the floor, with wolf cubs on her lap. More lazed beside her, with smiles of contentment on their faces. But it was not this that made Beck stare. It was the wolf fang that she wore around her neck.

She rose to her feet, and as she did so, she

seemed to grow, blossoming into a young woman. She held Beck in her arms and murmured in his ear, 'You came back, my little one.'

Beck realised that he was crying. He knew who she was, and it made him so angry. The wise lady of the forest. A shapeshifter, who loved humans and animals equally. And… and…

'You're my mother,' he said softly.

The wise lady nodded. She was crying too.

'Why did you leave me?' he yelled at her. 'Why did you never tell me?'

'Your place isn't with me, Beck,' she replied. 'You may be a human but your place is with the wolves. You know that. I had to show you your own life.'

'Why did you capture the wolf cubs?' Beck choked.

'I didn't. It was part of a…' she shuddered, 'breeding programme by the master of this house. When I found out, I got a job here so that I could try and help them. I saw the master fall in battle earlier today. He won't be bothering anyone again.' She smiled gently. 'Goodbye, Beck.' She shimmered and dissolved into a fine mist.

Beck slumped on the floor, his head reeling. But after a moment he could only hear one thing. The wolves calling him back to the forest.

Beth Cadwalladr, aged 11
Comberton Village College, Cambridgeshire

Red

by Bethany Foxon

As the cry of the wolf echoed over the forest, the fire went out and Beck was left in darkness. He reached for his knife, hurriedly shoved it in his backpack and started running... If only he could make it back to the cabin.

Stumbling over the gnarled roots of an oak, Beck glanced over his shoulder into the darkness. He froze, listening as a twig cracked in the distance, but the noise was lost as another wave of thunder rolled across the valley. This was the worst storm Beck could remember since Red had disappeared. Everyone had always called her Red on account of her long, coppery hair, and later the red coat that she would always wear. She loved that coat.

Another howl cut through Beck like a knife through water. It was definitely closer this time. Too close. He carried on through the darkness and left the path to take a shortcut lined with gorse and brambles. It was more suited to animals than boys, but it was the shortest route home.

Red had always hated this route; she never strayed from the path. No one really knows what happened to her. She was on her way to Granny's and never made it home. Old Mrs Lowe from the village near Granny's house said she saw a little girl in a red coat talking to a man. But Mrs Lowe was not exactly a reliable witness. Anyway, the mysterious man had not been seen again, and when Beck's father had reached the cottage, he had found Granny dead in her bed and not a trace of Red. There were large footprints around the cottage though...

A flash of lightning bathed the path silvery white as though the world had been cast into iron, then the darkness fell once more, a smothering blanket of nothingness. Panting, Beck paused for a moment, peering down the path into the gloom. If only there was a moon! He couldn't hear anything, and he certainly couldn't see anything, he just had a sort of feeling. Like he was being watched. As another flash of lightning lit up the area, a glimpse of red in the corner of his eye made him spin around, hand groping in his backpack for his knife. There was nothing there. A crack like a gunshot echoed through the trees behind him and he leapt round again, knife in hand. Nothing.

Then out of the darkness came a sound that made his blood freeze and his hands tremble. A soft giggle. Like that of a child. A little girl. Dropping the knife he lunged for the path, rolling upright and running before his feet hit the ground. A long, piercing howl sounded behind him, an animal scream of delight. It was hunting him...

After Red's disappearance, his father had transformed their cottage into a stronghold ready to withstand any attack. Then he'd gone out into the forest with his axe and never returned. But it was not his father's grief that had worried Beck; he had always loved Red so much more than him. It was his mother. Slowly, she had withdrawn further and further into herself until one day she had gone. Her body sat, rocking gently forwards and backwards by the fire in the cabin, but Beck's mother, the warm, funny and loving person, had gone forever.

Gasping for breath, he glanced over his shoulder into the gloom, listening. There was nothing but the sound of panting. His breath caught in his throat as an icy dread dripped down his spine, but the panting continued. It wasn't just hunting him; it was almost on top of him! As he ran, Beck could feel a warm breath on the back of his neck; hear the thud of heavy paws on the damp soil echoing his own footsteps. No matter how fast he ran it was always just a few paces behind. He could never outrun it. There was no escape. It was going to get him.

Suddenly the forest lit up in a flash of lightning and a dark shape was illuminated on the horizon. It was the house. Beck was safe! Sprinting the last few steps, he reached out for the handle, pulling at the latch... it stuck fast.

Frantic, he peered through the window. The bolt was drawn, sealing the door against the darkness, against the horrors of the night, against him. Pounding on the glass, he shouted to his mother. If she had managed to get up and bolt the door, could she manage to get up and unbolt it? With painful slowness, she turned from her seat by the fire, gazing at him with blank, dead eyes. For a moment she seemed puzzled, and then her eyes settled once more on something only she could see, and she turned away from him, back to the fire.

Beck pounded on the door, kicking and screaming, but his father had built the house to withstand wild storms and creatures like bears and wolves. The cabin that had sheltered and protected him for all these years turned its back on Beck. He was on his own... or perhaps not.

His back to the door, Beck stared in horrified fascination at the deep, golden eyes which gazed back at him from the trees. He pushed himself as far back into the door as possible, as a tiny figure not half his size emerged. She stepped into the light, pushing back her red hood and unleashing a mane of coppery hair which curled delicately round her face. She smiled, revealing rows of tiny, shark-like teeth and gazed at him with her dreadful eyes.

'Hello Beck,' she hissed. 'Did you miss me?'

'But, you're dead...' he whispered, 'the creature...'

She laughed with a menacing undertone. 'Am I? Then I suppose Father's dead as well, and the gypsy man, and the woman with the baby and all the others...' With each new name she spun around, becoming each person as she did so and smiling all the while. 'Or perhaps not quite dead, just part of something bigger...'

And Beck could only watch, paralysed with fear as the petite form of his baby sister transformed, changing until she was a monstrous creature with huge black paws, slavering jaws and mesmerisingly deep, golden eyes with a single dark slit through the centre. The last thing Beck knew was a glimpse of red hood, and a low snigger which rose into a long, piercing howl.

In the village, Brenda Drew leaned over the fence to Sally Long: 'Well, I heard that Beck, the boy from that family in the woods, he's been missing for months. His poor mother, bless her soul, had long since died and no one's seen the father for years.'

Sally frowned, puzzled. 'That's funny,' she said to her neighbour in confusion. 'My Tom's just gone off to the woods with a boy. I didn't recognise him at the time, but come to think of it he did remind me of Beck, though he was acting mighty odd. Strange eyes he had, too...'

Bethany Foxon, aged 15
Exmouth Community College, Devon

'**Better start running,**' he said with an **evil grin, patting the shrouded cage beside him. 'You**'ve got a thirty-second head start and then I let it out.'

Mark Walden

Fear

by James Norrington Hughes-Stanton

"'Better start running,' he said with an evil grin, patting the shrouded cage beside him. 'You've got a thirty-second head start and then I let it out.'
Luke froze in terror as he stared at the terrible creature, its dark yellow eyes fixed on his chest."

I snap the book shut, my heart pounding in my chest. Horror books always do that to me, but I read them anyway. I tell my friends I am fearless, but that is not exactly true. In fact it's the opposite. I am the easiest person to scare in the world, the universe. I would scream if I saw a plastic spider. No, the truth is that I am addicted to fear. It's like a drug. I hate it. The Fear, the Fear that makes my heart beat 200 times a minute, the Fear that makes me afraid of the dark, the Fear that even makes me check under my bed before I go to sleep. But I can't stop. The Fear will always be a part of me.

I glance sideways at the little digital clock on my bedside table, wondering how long I have before school. The little dial reads 02.47, four hours left. I won't get any more sleep, I reason, so I might as well read the new book. I always have a new one. Whether it is from the library or one of the town's book shops, I am never without one. My shelves are crammed with books, mostly horror, like 'Goosebumps', though here and there are the odd sci-fi or fantasy. I slowly open the dark, musty book again. It is rather an odd book, with no title or author on the back or front cover. In fact the only words not part of the story are part of the dedication. It reads, *"For those who want to feel fear."* Still it's a great story. It has everything a horror lover could want: demons, ghosts and death. Hideous deaths, torture, murder and pain. It definitely delivers what it promises. I've read adult books before, but none so gruesome. I smile and begin to read again.

"Luke turned and ran along the dark metal passageway. His feet slammed down on the cold floor in perfect unison with his heart..."

I look up. Did something just move? Probably nothing.

"'Run!' The thought pounded through Luke's head as he sped along the corridor. What could..."

I look up again. There! Something did move. I'm sure of it. I place the book down and walk to the door of my room, treading down as lightly as possible on the carpeted floor. I gaze out along the corridor, my eyes scanning the darkness, searching for anything out of place. I am sure that I have seen something, but what? My heart thumps in my chest. I go cold. I feel an odd sensation, as if someone is staring at my back, hungry, ready to pounce, ready to kill…

I spin round, and look back into my dusty bedroom. Was that a flash of colour? No, my room is empty. Nothing moves, nothing makes a sound. I have the same feeling in the back of my neck. The feeling of being watched. My head swings round again to face the empty hallway. I can't stand it any more. I dive back into my room and jump onto my bed. I turn again towards the door, leaning my back against the wall. Nothing can get me from behind then, and as I am watching the door, nothing can come through it. I sit and stare, my heartbeat gradually slowing, only diverting my eyes occasionally to glance at the small luminous clock, its numbers counting ever upwards. 03.37.

I need to read. It will steady my nerves. The Fear will be worse when I stop but I can't feel anything while I read. I open the book again. I lose myself in it, each page bringing new horror and peril, and time seems to stand still. At last, I turn the page to be confronted by the last chapter. A good place to stop. I look up at the clock, then down to the book again. Then I freeze. Slowly, I raise my head and stare at the little glowing numbers. 03.37, the same time as before. It must have stopped, but then why are the numbers lit up? It must just be the counting mechanism. I shiver, and that is when I hear it.

'Daniel!'

No, it can't be. I must be imagining it.

'Daniel, Daniel!' calls the soft voice again.

I look up and utter a muffled cry. Something's wrong. My brain has picked up on it, but for a split second, I don't know what it is. I don't want to know. But then I see it. Staring pointedly at me from the mirror above my chest of drawers is a grinning, terrifying face. It has yellow teeth and lumpy skin. And its eyes, its eyes are gaping black holes.

'Come here, Daniel, come here,' it calls to me. 'Come here.'

'No.' It takes all my willpower to utter the monosyllable.

The face smiles at me. 'Daniel, you don't have a choice.'

I find my legs moving, dragging me off the bed. 'No… no, please.'

'Come here, Daniel, come to me,' the face says in its calm, cool voice.

I find my hand rising, reaching out, reaching for the mirror.

'Let me out, Daniel, let me out.'

I can't stop. My fingers move closer and closer to the mirror.

'Now Daniel, now.' The voice sounds excited now, hungry. 'Let me out!'

My outstretched hand touches the mirror. It's ice cold. Suddenly, I regain control of my body, and stumble backwards, towards the door. But it is too late. The mirror screams. Suddenly shadows pour out of it, spilling onto the floor. I look up. In the centre of my room stands the man, the man in the mirror, next to a shrouded cage.

'Thirty seconds,' laughs the man.

The book, it is coming true!

'Go away,' I sob. 'You're not real. I don't believe in you.'

'Oh, but you do,' says the man, his empty eyes staring into my skull, dripping with malice. 'You made me from your fear,' he growls. 'I *am* your belief.'

He was right. What could I do?

'What do you want me for?' I manage to squeak.

'I don't want you, you want me. You want to feel Fear.'

It's true. Suddenly I know what I have to do. 'No,' I say. 'I don't.' I run, and grab the book, his book, from the table, and throw it as hard as I can at the mirror. It shatters, shards flying from the now empty frame. I hear a scream, so high-pitched I can't bear it.

I slowly open my eyes. My alarm clock is ringing. I sit up, and listen to my parents talking downstairs. A dream, that was all. I laugh inwardly as I stand up, just a stupid dream. Then I stop, horror-stricken as I stare at the mirror. The shattered mirror.

James Norrington Hughes-Stanton, aged 14
Ipswich School, Suffolk

Test Subject

by Andrew Myles

'Better start running,' he said with an evil grin, patting the shrouded cage beside him. 'You've got a thirty-second head start and then I let it out.'

I could hardly breathe. All of this for a small protest? I ran into a dark alleyway and caught my breath. I was in a bad situation. In this year of 2026 martial law had been declared and we had a new totalitarian government. Anyone who wasn't white or Christian was immediately suspected as a terrorist and could be carefully removed from existence with no trace. I was part of a small protest to save a forest and now I was acting as the government's guinea pig for their new 'advanced interrogation', which was a euphemism for torture.

The government had declared 2026 a new beginning, a year zero. It was suspected that drugs had been put in the water supply to keep the population in order but anyone with any evidence towards this fact would either mysteriously disappear or suddenly stop all research. Martial law was declared because global warming had caused massive flooding and the population started to panic and act out against the government.

I lived in a small village and had to be very careful about what I said or did, but when the government decided to cut down the forest and replace it with a 'behavioural repair facility' I had had enough. Loggers came and I stood in their way. I was immediately tranquilised. I didn't remember what happened next but I remember waking up in a room with a blindfold tied around my head.

At that point I was what the government called 'fair game', meaning I no longer had my rights and could be tested on as much as they wanted. I didn't know what they would do next; I thought I wouldn't see tomorrow. I was tied up there for a few hours without being given any food or water but eventually I heard some footsteps. A door opened and people came in. I couldn't tell how many people it was because of the blindfold but it sounded like two or three people.

My blindfold was quickly untied and I found myself facing two people; one seemed to be in the military and the other was in a white lab coat. They mumbled a few words to each other about the test seeming to be successful and then asked how my eyesight was; I replied saying it was fine. They then blindfolded me and led me to another room. They performed a series of tests on me and if I didn't comply I would be shot.

After the tests I was thrown into a room and my blindfold was untied. I was told I could sleep there. The room was completely white and sealed off. Everything had been taken from my pockets and I had no way of escaping. I decided that all I could do was sleep.

Sometime later I was awoken by a loud bang. My door was kicked open and two figures in black blindfolded me once again and I was brought to a room with a cage in the centre of it and a man standing over the cage.

I was standing in the alleyway; there wasn't much I could do next. If I somehow escaped I wouldn't be able to live a proper life, and if I was caught I would be brutally slaughtered. I decided to try and escape now and figure out my life later. I saw a manhole and quickly rushed down it. The sewers were dark and damp, there was ooze dripping from the walls and ceiling and it smelled horrible. It reminded me of the current situation in the world today.

I ran around a corner and heard a crashing sound; the thing from the cage stared me in the eyes. I was shocked by what I saw. It was a new breed of human: it had goggles on to cover its eyes, pale and cracked skin and a mouth sealed shut. It was almost symbolic of our new society. Partially blind, no possessions and no mouth to speak out with. I couldn't bear to think that this was once a human being. It had huge claws to tear apart flesh and I was guessing they were sharpened specially for me. I couldn't just stand there feeling sorry for my own personal angel of death so I kept running and went back up a different manhole.

There was a crowd of people around, and the army was marching. It looked like a parade, possibly to celebrate some unethical victory in a war. I darted into the crowd to try and blend in and escape, but the being that was chasing me had a heightened sense of smell since it could barely see and had no mouth, so it found me with ease.

I didn't know what to do next, all of the people ran away and the army continued to march as if it was all planned. I stepped back slowly until my back reached a brick wall. I could see the being coming closer and closer to me with each passing second. Its heavy breathing was getting louder as it drew closer. I thought if I was going down I might as well try and take it down with me. I lunged at the thing and it quickly thrust its claws through my torso.

I lay there, blood spewing from the wound; I saw a cross in neon lights, celebrities in posters with miscellaneous religious items attached to them as if they were some sort of fashion accessory; I knew I wasn't meant to be in this world; this world was commercial, controlled by the government, and everyone was blind as to what was going on. It was my time to go and despite what popular opinion said I wouldn't be going anywhere except rotting into the ground for all eternity, but it was better than rotting here on earth.

Andrew Myles, aged 14
Beech Hill College, County Monaghan, Ireland

The Gatekeeper

by Poppy Donaldson

'**Better start running,**' **he said with an evil grin, patting the shrouded cage beside him.** '**You've got a thirty-second head start and then I let it out.**'

Lottie grabbed my arm, turning to run, her voice tremulous with panic. 'C'mon Jess, let's get out of here!'

I pulled away from her grasp and turned on the gatekeeper. 'I'm not running anywhere,' I said, trying to sound both confident and defiant. 'I'm going to stand and fight whatever you have in there.'

I'm not sure who looked more surprised, the gatekeeper or Lottie. Her jaw had dropped, but in an instant she gathered her wits and hissed at me, 'Are you mad?'

I ignored her. A dozen questions were buzzing like angry wasps inside my head. For a start I half recognised the man with the cage, but I couldn't quite place him. I couldn't help thinking that he was one of the ground staff. I could have walked past him every day and never really paid him any heed until now. Nasty cold sore though.

'No,' I said absently to Jess, '… if you run from an animal it will always chase you. I learned that lesson in Africa. If you stand your ground then at least you have a chance.' I shivered as I remembered the occasion I had seen a lioness run down a zebra. We had no idea what was in the cage, but whatever it was, if we ran we wouldn't get past the gatekeeper.

It's not that I thought that we wouldn't be able to get away from the beast… we were both pretty quick on our feet, both forwards in our hockey team and quite swift around the lacrosse pitch. No, it wasn't that I doubted either of our running abilities in the least, but I certainly didn't want us to end up looking like that poor zebra.

Lottie looked really agitated now. 'Jess, for goodness sake, if you don't run you still get ripped to shreds, and we've only got 15 seconds!'

'No Lottie,' I said, 'we've got to face this thing… whatever it is. We don't actually know what he's got in there.'

Lottie glanced nervously at the cage, then at the scruffy, red-faced gatekeeper. He looked ordinary enough, harmless even.

The shock of being confronted by him was wearing off now. 'I reckon all he's got in there is a little fluffy guinea pig,' I suggested. We both giggled. It was ill judged.

The gatekeeper snarled at us, 'Ladies, I am

serious.' As if to add emphasis to whatever he had in the cage, he gave what I can only describe as a snickering giggle, and to my horror a black claw hitched up the bottom of the curtain to reveal a large rheumy eye staring straight at me.

'I think it fancies you,' commented Lottie, jumping behind me. Glutinous drool dripped from the cage and splashed on the concrete. The cage shook, but it was still difficult to judge what, or even how large, the creature was. The humour of the moment had certainly vanished, and I concentrated on trying to make sense of the situation.

'Whatever you've got in there we're still not running,' I told the gatekeeper and he seemed momentarily taken aback, but quickly composed himself, maintaining his aura of menace.

An idea was coming to me. 'Lottie, what is it they say about music?'

'Umm… it's the food of love?' she offered.

'No woman! Savage beasts…' I clicked my fingers in frustration. 'Music soothes the savage beast doesn't it? Do you listen at all in Latin?'

'Oh yeah,' said Lottie, 'give me a moment, I'll just whip out a cello from my backpack and play him a piece from 'Swan Lake', that should do the trick.'

'This is no time for your sarcasm!' I scolded her. 'Where's your iPod?'

'My iPod… it's – here.' She rummaged around in her blazer pocket producing a Mars Bar, two pencils and a hairbrush before pulling out her most prized possession, or her 'life support machine' as it had been referred to in a strict telling-off from Mrs McDougal last week.

'Great.' I took it from her. 'And the earphones?'

Lottie untangled them from around her collar, where they had been carefully hidden during lessons. There was no time to waste. I pressed play and, making sure that the volume was at its maximum, dangled it nervously in front of the cage. Neither of us had noticed that the gatekeeper had been counting. Not only that, but he was almost at zero.

'Three, two, one...' The word 'zero' had barely left his chapped lips before I heard the cage door fly up beneath the shroud with a loud metal clang. The gatekeeper's face transformed to a broken-toothed grin.

At first, nothing happened. I realised that Lottie had her eyes tightly shut and I couldn't help thinking that it might be wiser to keep them open. After a little while, it became clear to all three of us that the drooling animal had no intention of coming out. The gatekeeper's nasty grin had disappeared and he now looked rather disgruntled.

Jess nudged me with her elbow, pointing to the dark cloth that still covered the cage. The creature inside was apparently rocking from side to side in time with Pink and distinctly humming, just like a young child lulling itself to sleep in a cot. We looked at each other for a moment. I spotted a long branch by the wall, walked deliberately over and picked it up. Then, standing back, I lifted the cloth, revealing the ugly beast inside the cage. It was the size of a large dog, black and furry, somewhat simian in appearance, powerfully muscled with a flat gorilla-like face but hooked claws at the ends of its arms and legs. Whatever it was though, it was enjoying the song so much that it had rolled onto its back and started purring.

'Well done,' hissed the gatekeeper, 'you have passed the first test.' He turned a large iron key in the green door and swung it open on its hinges to allow us through the wall into the corridor beyond.

'Come on Jess,' said Lottie, nipping quickly through the doorway. 'If we don't hurry we'll get another punishment for being late.'

'Blimey!' I whispered to myself as we watched our flustered classmates hurrying in from different directions, some with scratched faces and tousled hair, some boys with their uniforms caked in mud. They had obviously met with tests of their own. 'I really don't know about this school. It's becoming harder to get to English lessons every day!'

Poppy Donaldson, aged 15
Malvern College, Worcestershire

When I woke up it was still dark and I knew straightaway that everything was different.

Jenny Valentine

Crazy Woman

by Alice Glebocki

When I woke up it was still dark and I knew straightaway everything was different. I woke slowly, rising gently from the blackness of sleep. Sound filtered into my ears: birds singing, pigeons arguing over crumbs, various early risers making their way down the street. I could smell exhaust fumes, even this early. I opened my eyes a crack, squinting against the scratchiness begging me to keep them closed. I shifted on the hard ground, rubbing my sore head. I sat up slowly and shook the water droplets from my hair. I watched them splatter around me, sinking without trace into the damp concrete.

'Christ,' I muttered, squeezing my eyes closed as black bubbles burst on my vision. I staggered as I stood up, grasping hold of the freezing wall beside me. My legs were completely dead and I was shaking with cold. I wanted to be at home, lying in a warm bed, not out here in the winter weather all alone. I was overcome with dizziness as I leant down to pick up my coat. I pulled it on, trying not to use my right arm, which hurt like hell.

I started wandering down the street to warm up, imagining my heels crunching in another time. It felt like it was a whole other life to me, but it was only the night before.

He had been so angry that I was late. Well he worries about me. I always knew he was protective. It's sweet. I love it about him. Imaginary snow settled around me as I tried not to think.

Crazy woman.

The night had started so well. A group of us, all going out for coffee. We'd talked for ages, and laughed so much, until eventually Josie had suggested moving on to a pub. One had led to another, that had led to another and so on and so on. We'd been to clubs too, I can't remember all the places. Guys had flirted with all of us, Josie had gone home with one of them. We tried to tell her it was a mistake but we were all drunk by this time and it did no good.

I'd never got drunk before. I'd never dared. I didn't mean to, but it just sort of happened. Hard not to when my friends kept dropping drinks in front of me. It got easier after about the fourth. I stopped worrying so much - but when I got home I knew he could tell, and I felt so sick. He kept asking me questions and I couldn't concentrate on what he was saying. My guard was low because of the alcohol, and in the end I snapped at him to shut up...

We've argued before, of course, but never as

bad as that. I had been so scared. So, so scared.

I shuddered in the cold and huddled into my collar. I remembered his words as my feet covered the ground.

Stupid cow.

He'd been so angry. I hadn't known what he was going to do, I just stared at him as he screamed at me. I felt so awful for upsetting him. I was paying such close attention that I should have seen his fist speeding towards my face, but I didn't. That bruise joined the many others I had gotten. I had so many excuses by now, walking into a door or falling over; tripping on a chair or falling out of bed. I had sobbed at him that I was sorry but now I wasn't sure if he would let me back. It was always the same, but this time it was worse.

Tears began to build up in my eyes as I thought of life without him, it was unbearable, unthinkable. How could I possibly be without him? How could I possibly live my life without him at my side?

I started to run, not caring where I was going, not knowing what I was running from. Not thinking of anything but how I could not lose him, could not ever be without him.

Braindead bimbo.

I choked on a sob, tears racing each other down my cheeks. My feet pounded on the floor, I was never going to stop, and I was going to run forever. I tripped over my own feet and fell straight into somebody. They caught me easily in their strong arms.

Wait a moment. I knew these arms. I knew them better than my own. He was here! He had come to find me! I threw my arms around him, my broken right arm throbbing. It was he who had broken it the night before but he hadn't meant to, it wasn't really his fault anyway because I fell onto it when I was dodging his fist and tripped on the coffee table. I buried my face in his chest and breathed in the sharp smell of his aftershave. I loved his smell so much. It always soothed me.

'Hey, babe,' he said softly, pulling back from me a little. He winced as he saw the bruise just below my eye. Cupping my face in his large hands, he gazed into my eyes and very gently wiped my tears away with his thumbs. 'It's alright,' he soothed. 'I'm here.'

'I love you,' I whispered. 'I love you. I love you so much.'

'I know you do,' he replied fondly, playing with my hair. 'You coming home, you crazy woman?' he added, flicking my nose gently.

Crazy woman, braindead bimbo, stupid cow…

The words echoed around my head and I was jerked into a painful reality, one I had been hiding from myself so as not to have to face up to it.

He didn't love me. I adored him, would die for him, but he didn't love me in the slightest. I hated the very thought of it but I knew I was living in denial.

'Babe? You coming home then?'

I stared at him, seeing him from the outside for the first time.

'No,' I whispered.

And ran.

Alice Glebocki, aged 15
The Kimberley School, Nottinghamshire

Memories of my Past

by Rebecca Hardy

When I woke up it was still dark and I knew straightaway that everything was different. My bedroom wasn't right. I remember painting it purple with Dad, but somehow it had turned baby pink. It was like that when I was a baby. Pink with little stuffed animals everywhere. A tiny white cot sat in the corner. There was a little pink and white blanket lying in there. Everything was the same. Nothing was different, even the sign on the door. *Abby*, in little pink writing, I still have that on my door now. I didn't recognise the rest of the house, but it was definitely my house. There were pictures of me all over the place. There were voices, coming from the kitchen, a woman and a man.

'Mom, Dad, is that you?' I could only manage a whisper.

'Hello darling, let's get you some breakfast.'

'Err, no thanks, I'm not hungry.'

Mom grabbed a bowl off the counter and walked away from me. I walked further into the kitchen. There was a pink highchair there. There was a laugh, kind of squeaky, babyish.

'Come on now Matt, put her down. She won't eat anything otherwise.'

'Come on Abby, breakfast time!' Dad, he was holding a baby, me. He put me in the highchair. I was wearing a little purple babygrow, with little matching socks. I had dark brown, curly hair like Mom. I tried to stop myself but I couldn't. I went up to Mom and Dad and gave them both a kiss on the forehead. I felt like I would never be able to do that ever again. I didn't know what was going on but I hoped the moment would never end.

Everything was fading, no... Please, wait.

I was in the living room. Mom was sat on the sofa and I was in her lap. Dad came in and sat next to Mom, putting his arm around her. I was playing with the house keys. I dropped them on the floor. My parents didn't seem to notice. So I crawled out of Mom's lap and sat on the floor. For some strange reason, I turned around, grabbed hold of the sofa and stood up. I gradually let go and I started walking.

'Matt, Matt!' Mom was screaming. 'Matt, Abby, look she's walking.' Mom started bawling like a little baby.

'Come here Angel.' Dad got up and ran up to me. He looked like he was going to kill me; he was kissing me wildly, like he was never going to release me. Mom got up too, still crying her eyes out. She hugged Dad like there was no tomorrow.

I'd always wanted to see this moment. The first time I ever walked. It was so uplifting to see that. It was truly amazing. I've always imagined what happened, suppose everyone does really. I just imagined that Mom and Dad kept asking me to try and walk. I have never seen Mom and Dad smile so broadly.

No, not again, everything was going away from me…

Now I was sat in the same highchair, in the kitchen, with Mom. Dad must have been at work. Mom had her phone out and was recording me. She was tickling me, which was making me laugh.

'Mommy's tickling you. Yes she is, yes.'

'Momma.'

Mom's eyes lit up. She kissed me on the forehead and ran off to the hallway without saying a word.

'Matt, she said Momma, Abby said Momma.'

Wow, why is it so cold? Wait, how come we're outside? Just a second ago I was in the kitchen.

I turned around and there was my old primary school. Mom and Dad were holding one of my hands. I was in a little black skirt with grey tights. A little pink coat was zipped up tight. A purple book bag was in Dad's other hand and a lunchbox was in Mom's. It must have been my first day, Mom was crying, again. The bell rang and Dad let go of my hand, kissed me on my cheek and looked at Mom. He started giggling. She looked petrified. More scared than what I was.

'It's okay. Let her go Louise. She'll be fine.'

Mom slowly let go of my hand and she kissed me too. I skipped off happily towards the door. I looked back and waved, and then everything was gone.

We were sat on tiny blue chairs in the school hall. It was snowing outside. The stage was set up to look like a stable. I was on the stage in a little white dress, holding a doll. I was Mary, holding Baby Jesus. It was my first school play. The narrator started talking. I looked innocently at Mom and Dad and gave them a little wave. All the audience gave a little sigh.

Everything went black; I fell off the chair I was sat on. I heard people asking me if I was alright. I opened my eyes and we were still in the hall. Mom and Dad were crouching over me. This was it. The last chance I would ever get to speak to Mom and Dad. I knew it.

'This may sound strange but something terrible happened.' I couldn't go on. Tears began to stream from my eyes.

'No darling, everything's going to be alright.' It was Mom.

'We've called for help.' Trust Dad, he always relied on help.

'No, you don't understand. Please listen. This is my last chance I can say this.' Darkness was coming. I had to hurry. 'Please. I need to say this. Goodbye, I will always miss you.'

That was it. Darkness. Pain, excruciating pain.

There was music. I turned around, and there was my local church, St. Michael. I opened the doors and slipped in. *The Voice Within* by Christina Aguilera was playing.

'*Young girl don't cry, I'll be right here when your world starts to fall...*'

I remember telling Mom and Dad that at my funeral I wanted that song played. We were deciding what to play at my nan's funeral. I just said that joking. There were photos of me. My friends and family were sat down, all crying. Mom was holding my blanket. The same one from my cot. There was a coffin on a table at the front, with a picture of me on top. This was for me. All of it.

No, again, darkness. No it can't end like this. It can't.

It's true what people say. Before you die your life really does flash before your eyes.

Rebecca Hardy, aged 13
Hillcrest School, Birmingham

The moment I saw him, I just knew... Casey Clark was nothing but trouble.

Cathy Cassidy

Redemption

by Megan McGeown

The moment I saw him, I just knew... Casey Clark was nothing but trouble. I recognised him instantly, those brown, moody eyes. They bored right through me: I clearly meant nothing to him anymore. Did he even recognise me? Embarrassed for staring, I quickly busied myself with my shopping, as the train guard shook his head impatiently.

Casey's hair looked like it hadn't been washed since the last time I had seen him all those years ago – on that tragic night. Leather biker boots hugged his calves and a worn leather jacket finished his look off perfectly. This was clearly a man that always got his own way and was definitely not to be messed with. His eyes were drained of any compassion or love and his face was hard and aggressive. Time had not been kind to Casey Clark. His face was covered in lines and his belly was noticeably heavier. However, despite all these changes this was still the boy that I had loved all those years ago.

As children, Casey and I had been inseparable. We were neighbours, he had lived next door to me. We had been the best of friends and had done everything together. Throughout primary school we had been the ones to chatter at the back of the class and stick up for each other in the playground. When we moved up to junior school we were still as close as always. We would share the answers to test papers and run the races together on sports day. When Casey's sister was born with autism we vowed to stay the best of friends forever.

However this all changed when we moved up to secondary school. Casey had always been far more adventurous than me whilst I had been the academic one. This new school was far bigger than previously. No longer were we in the same classes and soon our friendship slowly dwindled. I was fixated on my work whereas Casey would centre his life around sport and parties. Our lives were taking completely different paths and it looked like they would never cross again.

I watched as Casey barged his way through the floods of innocent tourists and commuters. His eyes darted malevolently around the train station as he hunched down into one of the empty benches. I watched as he picked up a free magazine and tossed it back onto the floor, irritated. My heart was racing and the palms of my hands were getting sweaty. The words that he had screamed at me all those years ago were being repeated in my head over and over again. Why could I never forget what had happened?

When I was 15 I began volunteering at the

centre for disabled youths. It was there that I began to rekindle my friendship with Casey. His sister regularly attended the centre as her mother found it hard to cope with her behaviour and give the full attention that she needed. Casey and I laughed at the things we had done when we were younger and became friends. Soon I became infatuated with him and got angry when he couldn't come to the centre, and became envious of him loving his sister.

It was a mild, breezy night when I asked Casey to come with me for a walk down to Bushy Croft Reservoir. As children we had spent hours down at the reservoir, building dens and rafts and generally having a laugh. This was the night that I was planning on finally revealing my feelings to him. Yet things weren't going my way; Casey had brought his sister along to join us. We strolled down to the lake, bathing ourselves in the bright setting sun and enjoying the fresh air. Little could we have guessed the tragedy that was to unfold.

Kerry, Casey's sister, was demanding his full attention and so I suggested that we leave Kerry just for a minute whilst we wandered off. Casey hastily agreed as I took his hand and tempted him onto the beach, just out of sight of Kerry. At this moment I wasn't thinking about the safety of Kerry or the compromise that I was forcing Casey to make. Suddenly we heard a sound.

Casey dropped me and raised his head in alarm. It had been a choked scream and a heavy splash. We hurried over with my heart thumping and my voice too choked to even utter a word. Casey screamed Kerry's name again and again before ripping off his shirt and wading his way into the lake's depths. Heavy tears were rolling down his cheeks and his face was warped with utter despair. I was frozen in fear and a million thoughts were tearing throughout my mind. A minute passed as I watched Casey search for his sister under the water's surface. Finally, after what seemed hours, he had found what he was looking for and brought his sister's limp body up to the pebbled beach.

The clock in the train station was ticking and still I had not worked out what to do. I was still closely watching Casey, secretly hoping that he would catch my eye and recognise me. That he might come over to me, remember our old friendship and forgive me, so that I could finally get on with my life and accept the guilt that has wrought my existence for these past years. Unsurprisingly Casey didn't even acknowledge me.

Soon after Kerry's body was lifted from the water an ambulance and paramedics appeared at the scene. They had to persuade Casey to let go of his younger sister's body and then carry it into the ambulance. Casey sat there sobbing at the edge of the impossibly still lake whilst his heart was breaking. I viewed this desperate scene and observed as the paramedics explained to Casey that they had been unable to resuscitate his sister. This was when the anger began. He came over to me, his face bright red and his eyes swarming with hatred.

'You killed my sister,' he spat at me, 'and for that I shall never forgive you!'

That was the last time that I ever spoke to Casey as I soon moved away to university and busied myself with a whole new group of friends. However, all my life I have been haunted by those tragic memories.

Finally, this was my chance to seek redemption. The train had pulled in and now was my chance. Casey stood up and was racing towards the train within the swarms of other passengers. I caught him and urgently grabbed his arm but he just shook me off without even looking at me and strode onto the carriage. I wept as the train doors closed and I was left on the platform. The train was slowly picking up speed until the last carriage had disappeared into the blackness of the tunnel. I was crying so uncontrollably that I was now on the platform's cold, concrete floor. Suddenly my heart leapt. On the other side of the rail track I saw the huge figure of my childhood friend with the faint outline of a smile etched on his face.

He mouthed one phrase before wandering back into the crowds of this busy London train station. It was just three words:

'I forgive you.'

Megan McGeown, aged 13
Oxted School, Surrey

Runaway Love

by Hannah Court

The moment I saw him, I just knew... Casey Clark was nothing but trouble.

So why, why, *why* didn't I just stay *away*?

I can see my reflection in a shop window. My hair, knotted and tangled, my lips, my whole body, torn and bleeding, and my legs are every shade of violet, indigo and plum. My clothes are ripped open. All this for a boy with floppy hair and emerald eyes.

Casey Clark. The boy of my dreams. The boy of my nightmares.

Once, I was happy. It seems centuries ago, now. That's what it was like with Casey. Seconds were hours, and the minutes were forever. He made time stop, as well as my heart. My heart that is now heavy with love, hate, and shame. I gave up everything I had, and more, just for him.

It was Halloween night and I'd lost my sister Myrna trick or treating. I wasn't too bothered. She was 18 and could look after herself, but it was freezing and I didn't know the way back to her flat. I carried on knocking on doors asking if anyone had seen a half-angel, half-devil about so high. On the umpteenth door, a boy answered. He was about five years old and had chocolate drool dribbling down his pyjamas. Yuck! I asked him if he had seen my sister and he started babbling on about how he'd seen 35 witches and 20 devils and 16 vampires and nine ghosts but *I'm* his first dark angel. Then he said am I trick or treating and he said I've got Twixes and Milky Ways and Dairy Milks and lollipops and would-I-like-a-Mars-Bar and God knows what else.

That was the moment Casey walked down the stairs. He was rubbing a towel on his wet hair and was wearing a pair of damp pyjama bottoms, with no top on! My heart leapt into my throat and starting pumping the tango. He came to the door and looked me up and down. All of a sudden I felt very self-conscious. I was wearing black, patent, just above the knee high-heeled boots, black tights and a tight, shiny leather dress, with a pair of black fluffy angel wings and a glittery black halo. When me and my sister had found this in *Claire's* it was really funny and she said I looked amazing in it, especially with her Goth mate's black boots. Since when did I trust *my* sister? She was a total prankster. You could see all my lumps and bumps in that goddamned dress.

In the end, I ended up sitting in his living room, eating Domino's pizza with him and his little brother. He had a deep, smooth voice, and when he looked at me his eyes drank me in. They were like the ocean, sea green and sparkling, going on forever.

It was that sparkle that lured me in. That mischievous side of him. That was when I fell in love.

The house was beautiful, and when I told him so he laughed.

'Funny you should think so, we only moved in a week ago!' he exclaimed. 'I'm looking forward to school on Monday, I'm going to Queensmere Comprehensive, do you know it?'

'Only a lot! I've gone there since I was eleven! I'm in year nine now, what year are you?'

'Same! It would be funny if we were in the same form, wouldn't it! I'm in 9ZK. Mr Kennedy...'

Yeah, hilarious. And it was, for the first couple of weeks. Me and Casey started going out, two days after he started. I was ecstatic.

Dear Marcie

I think you're drop dead gorgeous, and if you wouldn't mind, would you go out with me?

Casey xxx

Oh, he was a charmer, and I thought I was the luckiest girl on Earth. Marcie Keener, going out with the boy all the girls fancied. Even the boys said he was fit! It was three weeks after he started Queensmere Comp. It was 9.30pm and I was watching the X Factor, when the doorbell rang.

Mum and Dad were out, going to some stuffy meeting. I opened the door, it was chucking it down with rain. Casey was soaked to the skin and looked like he was bawling his eyes out.

73

'Casey? Casey! What, what happened? Are you okay?' I ran my hand through his dripping hair. I screamed. My hand was covered in blood.

'Casey! You're bleeding! Quick, come inside!'

'No, Marcie, please, you have to come with me!' He yanked my arm. I was on my knees, he closed the door.

'Casey, what are you doing?' I wailed. My knees were covered in blood, because there was glass on the front step. I was only wearing my too-small Little Miss Chatterbox nightie, which barely covered my knickers, and now it was soaking wet it clung to me and rode up my legs. He pulled my right arm and started heaving me down the street.

'Casey, stop, you're hurting me! Please, Casey, please, where are we going? Casey, stop, stop, Casey please!' I screamed 'CASEY!'

It was now me who was bawling my eyes out. By the time we got to Chester Avenue I had given up trying to stop Casey dragging me to wherever Casey was dragging me to. Tears blurred my vision, and I could just make out Casey had brought me to some kind of field. It was late November and it was freezing. He thrust me into some woods and pushed me down on the floor, scraping my bare thighs on the jagged forest floor.

Even then, terrified of what Casey was going to do with me, it didn't stop me loving him.

'C-c-c-Casey? Are you okay? Are you hurt? Is that why I'm here? To help you?' I said, grasping at straws.

What seemed like eternity later, he spoke.

'I need you. You are my fuel. You keep me going. My life, it was hopeless, empty before I met you, Marcie.' He looked at me, his eyes wet. 'My dad, he sells houses. That house, that I live in, is one that Dad's selling. I'm going, Marcie, my dad's making us go and live in Florida. And I can't do it. So I'm running away. With you, Marcie. I'm sorry I hurt you. I, I love you Marcie.'

He took me in his arms and we kissed. I could taste his salty tears and it took us away from a grubby wood, to a dreamland, where anything was possible. I was floating on cloud nine, I was flying, and it was the best sensation in the world.

So, that's where we are now, living in ditches, and fields and on street corners under sheets of cardboard.

I still wish I had fought harder that night. I still wish I hadn't opened that door. And how I wish that when that little boy answered that door and was going on about witches and Milky Way bars I just took a lollipop and went on to find Myrna.

I hate Casey for what he's done to me.

But most of all I love him for what he's done for my empty heart.

Hannah Court, aged 12
William Allitt School, Derbyshire

The witch placed two mysterious objects on the table and now I had to choose: one would free me, one would kill me, but both were too terrible to touch!

Joe Delaney

Witch's Story

by Emily Stanford

'The witch placed two mysterious objects on the table and now I had to choose: one would free me, one would kill me, but both were too terrible to touch!'

I can almost imagine in my head that is what he would say to his friends if he got home, trying not to remember the fear he felt. I can see the pain that has overcome him in making this decision. He needs to know the truth but I cannot tell him. His beautiful brown eyes have been taken over by fear and he is shaking uncontrollably. His black hair is plastered to his face, that is as pale as new fallen snow.

This curse was not just upon me now, I had placed it upon him too. I had to work with it for nine years but now I had put this burden upon him without his knowledge. It was placed upon me on my fifteenth birthday by an evil witch who said that on my twenty-fifth birthday, if I had not found my saviour, I would die a painful and lonely death. Now I only have a matter of months left.

There is more I suppose you should know

about this curse. Firstly, this curse means I am trapped in an old woman's body until the day I am freed. If I am not freed I will die in this body on the day I turn 25. Secondly, I have to find the person with the purest soul and they must choose the object that will free me, but if they pick the wrong one I will die anyway. The only problem is there is only one with a pure soul in every generation and I have to find the one within mine. And lastly, once I have found the one with a pure soul I cannot tell him of his purpose but must tell him that if he chooses the correct object *he* will be freed but if he chooses the wrong one *he* will die. If I attempt to tell him that this is not the case he will be shot down with an incredible torturing pain.

All these years I have been walking around in this old body whilst my young soul has been fighting to get out.

The first time I saw him I knew he was the one I needed. I had been looking for nine long years and then I found him. As I walked past the many market stalls, I took a glance back at the crowds behind me: one man stood out and I could no longer see everyone else.

I needed a quiet place, all I could think of whilst walking around the corner was him and if he could be the one to save me. Was he the pure one I had waited for? Or was I just looking too hard as my time was slowly running out? I took a deep breath and turned back to the swarming crowds to go home. As I re-entered the crowd I crashed into a man of my own age, but in my eyes he was glowing, glowing with a white light effect. Could I be mad? As he stooped to pick up my bags and offered to carry them home for me I saw he was the one I had seen behind me moments earlier.

When I opened my door, I turned to look at him. He was the only person from this entire town that stopped to help an old lady with her shopping. He radiated kindness and love and I had no doubt I would be freed. As I locked the door of the room I kept him in I felt great shame and remorse. I would free him soon, but just then I could not lose him.

It has now been a week and I have been watching him in the room. He is becoming weak, he will not eat and sleeps all of the time. I see him stare longingly at the food I slide under the door but not quite trusting me not to poison him. Why would I want to damage his sweet, brave face?

Tomorrow is the day that has slowly been creeping up on me. All through the night I tossed and turned as I was tortured by visions of him in the room I trapped him in, alone and scared, and the moment I could not avoid. I wanted to go in and tell him why I had done this but I couldn't. Why would he believe me, someone who had betrayed his trust?

It has all been building up to this moment:

him, me and the objects that could save my life or in turn destroy it. He thinks I wanted this and that I arranged it so I could torture him, but he does not see I need him and will try my best to keep him safe. I will not blame him if he chooses the wrong one as I could not have done any better than him.

I watch him, pale and in a cold sweat. How could I have done this to him? He reaches out to one object. But then changes his mind and pulls back his hand. We are in the simple room I put aside specifically for this moment. There is just a simple table with a chair facing it and a few candlesticks dotted around the room. The two objects are upon the table, exactly the same as the first day they appeared there. They both attract you but also repel you at the same time.

As I wait I cannot help but feel he is going to make the wrong choice even though I know I should be trusting him. I begin to wander the room trying to bury the feelings of dread building up inside me. As I have my back to him I feel a knife pain shoot through my spine and I let out a scream. My skin begins to bubble and burn. I can no longer see anything but pitch blackness. Suddenly, all I can feel is a soft touch on my wrist and I hear him whispering to me, although I cannot make out what he is saying. He gasps and I can no longer feel his hands on me. Then, nothing.

I wake up on my bed and look at my hands.

I am young again! I leap out of bed and look at myself in the mirror and everything is back to how it should be at this age. My wrinkles are gone and my hair is no longer grey! Then I see him at the door smiling at me and I begin to laugh. As I walk over to him I am overcome with love for him. As we share an affectionate embrace I know he is the one I was looking for to save me, and so much more.

Emily Stanford, aged 13
St. Neots Community College, Cambridgeshire

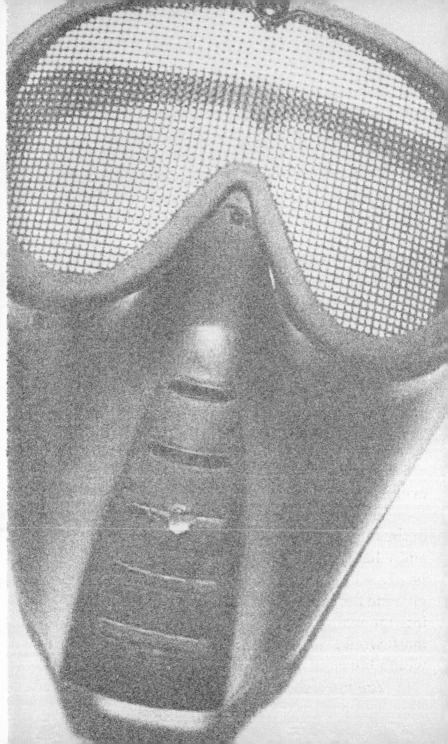

The Mask of Time

by Emily Pritchard and Hanna Tillmann-Morris

'The witch placed two mysterious objects on the table, and now I had to choose; one would free me, one would kill me, but both were too terrible to touch!'

So there they were. Lying either side of me, giving off a dim glow just enabling me to identify them in the suffocating darkness of the cave. The witch leaned over me, her once-beautiful face marked with age, pain, and sorrow, her eyes aglow like red-hot embers against the coal blackness around her. But somehow she didn't scare me. There was something about her that seemed familiar… I understood her in almost every way.

She didn't even have to explain the meaning of the objects – I already knew what they were, and what they would do. On my right, a long, pearly-white glove with black satin lining would give me the power to climb out of the cave, back into the real world. On my left, a death-black mask would turn me so old and weak that I would have but a few minutes to live.

'You must choose,' the witch rasped.

I knew what the obvious choice was: the glove that would take me home to…

And that was the point. I had nothing to go back for. Ever since my much-loved older sister, on whom I had always depended, had gone missing, my life had started to go downhill. Grief stricken, my parents split up, and as I moved into my new school, alone and afraid, I became an easy victim for bullies like Sean Harrison and his cronies, thugs who could drive you to despair just for a bit of 'fun'.

So what *was* the point of going back? I might as well die and not have to endure the humiliation of being a poor sad boy, a 'loser' who couldn't stand up to anyone.

But wasn't it even more sad-boy loserish to just *give up* and not fight back like a proper boy with a proper grip on the world? No! Giving up was not good enough! I would put on the glove and face my problems with courage!

I reached across to where the glove lay and snatched it up. With a last defiant glare at the witch, I pulled on the glove, and looked around for the way out. The witch pointed upwards. Following her gaze, I craned my neck to see a thin sliver of light, which seemed at least a hundred feet above us. But the glove gave me a burst of unnatural strength, and I began climbing the towering wall of rock before I even knew what I was doing.

When I reached the top I looked down and

saw, in the witch's eyes, a distant memory, a fleeting image of…

Wait! This was no witch: it was my dear sister, Emma!

As the stone rolled over, blocking the entrance, she called up to me, 'You made the right choice, Alex!'

Then she was gone. But perhaps I could still save her?

I raced back to our cottage on the hillside for a spade as fast as I could, not wanting to lose any time. However, back at home, another surprise awaited me, for sitting at the kitchen table were my parents. Together.

I hadn't seen them together for nearly two years.

'Hello Alex!' said Mum, 'Would you like to sit down?'

I sat down. 'What is it?' I asked impatiently, desperate to get back. Mum and Dad glanced at each other.

'Alex, your mother and I have been talking. And, well… we've decided to give it another go. We're going to move up to the country – away from bad memories. A fresh start and all that…'

They looked at me, their faces eager but slightly nervous.

'No!' I yelled, jumping up from my chair.

We couldn't move – Emma wouldn't be able to come back! She was going to – I knew it. I shouted, raved, sulked, moaned, did everything

I could, but they would not change their minds. Two adults against one child – we were moving, and that was final.

So that was how, several months later, I found myself wandering aimlessly on a strange beach in an unfamiliar village on a weird coastline that was not our home.

I was bored, hungry, and cold, and it was about to rain. Miserably, I kicked a stone.

All at once, it triggered lots of other stones, and a great pile of them began crashing down, sinking into the sand.

Before I knew what was happening, rocks and sand slipped away under my feet and I was falling, falling…

As Alex fell down towards me for the second time, I felt a mixture of regret and guilty relief. I had hoped so much that my little brother wouldn't ever find me again and live a happy life that I could watch in my mind fondly until we both died together.

It was now with pity and horror that I looked at my little brother as he summed up all the courage he had – he never had much of it, bless him – to put that dreadful mask on his young face. With a despairing heart, and too weak to even speak, I watched the mask leer up at him mockingly.

'The right choice is different this time, Emma,' he whispered, understanding my feelings and thoughts. 'It's your turn to live now.'

What was he talking about? He was only thirteen; he'd had hardly what you'd call a fair turn to live.

But the choice was not mine. I watched with a broken heart as Alex reached out once more with a hand that I wished was gloved. As he picked the mask up, trembling with fear, I felt a shiver go down both of our spines. Then he placed it on his face.

At first, nothing happened, and then with a jolt I was pulled backwards through time; past distant memories, past ages, past happenings, past years. And meanwhile, I felt my strength returning, my health and beauty restoring, my spark reigniting. I started remembering how it was to be young again, but not enjoying it. Because of what was happening to my brother, in the corner.

I rushed over to where he lay dying, and cradled his head in my arms to ease my pain, tears silently streaming down my face. He smiled wearily up at me.

'Don't worry, Emma,' he told me, his voice rough and hoarse, 'I meant you to be free.'

'My dear little brother,' I sobbed in return, unable to express my grief in words.

The last thing he felt before he died was my kiss and my tears on his wrinkled cheek.

My first breath of fresh air was like magic to relieve my chest of the weight it had been bearing for the previous two years, and when I saw my parents our hearts lurched with joy, although the family would never be complete.

'But where's Alex?' they asked.

I couldn't tell them everything, but now I understood the spell woven round brother and sister.

'He is not gone forever,' I said.

**Emily Pritchard, aged 12 and
Hanna Tillmann-Morris, aged 11
Oxford High School, Oxfordshire**

Illustrations by Katy Jenkins, Age 13, Buckler's Mead Community School, Somerset.

Notes and ideas for future stories